A Bed of Stars

To Danny and Valentine

First edition 2023

Library of Congress Catalog Card Number 2022936748
ISBN 978-1-5362-1239-6

23 24 25 26 27 28 APS 10 9 8 7 6 5 4 3 2 1

Printed in Humen, Dongguan, China

This book was typeset in Athelas.
The illustrations were done in watercolor, gouache, and ink.

Candlewick Press
99 Dover Street
Somerville, Massachusetts 02144

www.candlewick.com

A Bed of Stars

JESSICA LOVE

CANDLEWICK PRESS

It used to be, when it was time for bed, I would imagine
the whole universe stretching on endlessly, forever.
The bigger it got, the smaller I felt. I was too worried
to fall asleep.

One morning at breakfast, my dad says, "We're going camping, you and me."

"Where?" I ask.

"The desert," says Dad.

"Why?" I ask.

And Dad says, "To shake hands with the universe."

We have an old truck named Darlin', and we pack her up with everything we'll need. The most important thing about packing is to put the big stuff in first, and then you can squeeze the small stuff in around it.

We drive out of the city, which smells like rubber and french fries, and listen to Dolly Parton sing.

As we climb up into the mountains, the smell changes
to sweet and smoky.

"This is my best smell," I say.

"Mine too," Dad says.

We drive over a mountain covered in charred black trees and also a lot of flowers.

Dad tells me all their names and what they are useful for.

Mountain Flowers

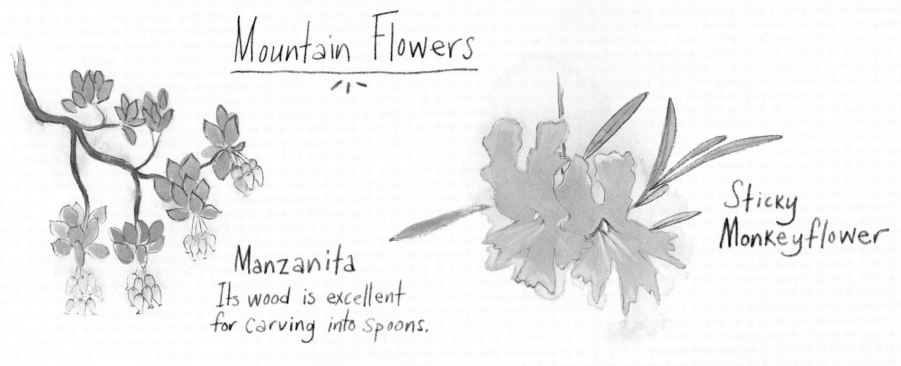

Manzanita
Its wood is excellent for carving into spoons.

Sticky Monkeyflower

White Sage

Ceanothus
Its seeds germinate after forest fires, and its flowers smell like boiling honey.

We stop at our favorite junkyard to see if there are any new parts for Darlin' and so Dad can "shoot the breeze" with Jodi. "Shooting the breeze" is when adults have a boring conversation.

I climb a tire mountain and draw a picture of Jodi's dog, who doesn't do anything except sleep.

When it's time to go, we drive away listening to the blues.

"This song is lonesome," I say to Dad, "but in a nice way."

Dad smiles and squeezes me closer.

Finally Dad brings Darlin' to a stop and says, "We're here."

"We're where?" I ask. "We're all alone."

"Not quite," says Dad.

The ground is covered in tiny tracks. Dad says they're the footprints of all the beetles who come out in the morning to drink the dew.

"The first thing to do," Dad says, "is jump in the sand dunes."

We lie back in the sand and name all the birds we can see. Dad says if he could be any bird, he'd be a crow, because they're smart and can use tools. If I were a bird, I'd be a swallow, because they can fly the hardest patterns.

Birds of the Desert

Turkey Vulture

Hawk

Crow

Cliff Swallow

The next thing to do is set up camp and build a fire.

How to Build a Fire

1. Gather fuel.

2. Arrange some rocks.

3. Light your sticks.

4. Then blow.

5. Sit around the fire and sing all the songs you know.

When the sun starts to set, we lie on Darlin' and watch the colors change.

"If there is a sunset," I say, "you have to stop and watch."

We each pick a spot in the sunset to live. They are right next to each other.

Then it's time to go to sleep.

"This is the part I'm scared of," I say. "How big the universe is and how it goes on and on forever."

After a minute, Dad says, "Do you know what stars are made of?"

"What?" I say.

"Energy," he says. "Same as you. Same as the beetles and crows and coyotes. We're all friends and family. Maybe if you learned their names, they wouldn't feel so much like strangers."

So we snuggle up all cozy, and we name all the stars we can see. We name some of them after folks we met today: Jodi's Dog Star, the Coyote Cluster, and the Beetle Nebula. I name one after me, too. It's not that I feel bigger or the universe feels smaller; it's more like I know we are made of the same stuff, but in different bodies. I fall asleep.

When we wake up the next morning, the sun is just tipping over the tops of the mountains.

"The first thing to do," I say to Dad, "is to drink hot chocolate in bed."

So we do.

As the sun climbs higher in the sky, we see that the desert has bloomed.
We say hello: ocotillo, globemallow, agave.

It's a long drive home, so we pack everything up, pour water on our firepit to make sure it is out, and check twice that we haven't left anything behind.

"Just footprints," Dad says.

"Like the beetles," I say.

As we drive back up into the mountains, Dad asks me to name all the new friends I've met, and I do: Beetles, Cacti, Coyotes, Stars . . .

And then we're back home! Mom is there with the baby, and I'm happy to see them.

"I have so many things to tell you," I say to the baby.

"We've got something for you, too," Mom says.

Covering my walls and ceiling are a million stars. Mom spent all day putting them up while we were gone.

"Whoa," I say.

It's like the whole universe is in my little bedroom.

That night, alone in the dark, I name all the stars: Mouse Star, Pine Tree Constellation, Sand Dune Galaxy, Darlin' Nebula. I fall asleep inside my house with my mom and dad and the baby nearby, and above me and below me and all around me are all my friends and family.

And I am at home in the universe.